WHO'S AT THE DOOR?

JC BRATTON

BLUE
MILK
Publishing

Who's at the Door?

By JC Bratton

ISBN: 978-0-9986453-1-5 (Paperback)

ISBN: 978-0-9986453-2-2 (e-book)

Library of Congress Control Number: 2019920002

First printing edition, January 2020

Second printing edition, May 2020

Third printing edition, November 2022

Blue Milk Publishing: San Jose, California

bluemilk.co

PROLOGUE
MAY 20, 2017

My head was spinning as I heard the sirens around me. I could feel the blood drip from my forehead, and I couldn't move my left leg. There were lights around me as I laid on a gurney. Apparently, I had hit something or *someone*. I just remember being tired after a long night. We just graduated, and I was at Shelly's late-night party. I had a fight with Mark. It started raining when I hit the road, and it was very hard to see.

"Miss, I'm Sheriff King. I know things may be a bit fuzzy, but can you tell me what happened?" The Sheriff had a sympathetic look on his face as he hovered over me.

"I — I can't remember. Did I hurt someone?" I asked.

"No, Miss; just one big dent on your front bumper from you hitting that tree over yonder. Looks like you weren't drinking, which is good. Did you get distracted somehow?"

A tree? Distracted? Something distracted me, but I just don't remember what.

"I'm sorry, Sheriff, I am not sure," I struggled to talk, as

I was in so much pain. "I do remember being tired. I guess I must have drifted off the road."

I remember a feeling; a feeling of being frightened. It wasn't the fear of hitting a tree. It was a ghastly fear, something that tears into your soul...

CHAPTER ONE

"Bye, Jamie! We'll text you as soon as we land."

I waved good-bye as they climbed into the car. Mom always wanted to go to Hawaii, and Dad was finally able to break free from his robotics research company long enough to take Mom on her dream vacation for their 20th anniversary. They were such a cute couple: Dad was 6 feet, 4 inches tall and Mom was barely 5-feet. I met them in the middle at 5 feet, 7 inches with long brown hair and large brown eyes.

When I closed the door, the house felt a bit cold, but I was glad to have it to myself for the next 2 weeks. It's been about a month and a half since my accident, and now I am in a walking boot. I didn't feel that I was in any condition to enjoy Hawaii with Mom and Dad. They wanted to cancel the trip, but I vehemently said no. It was their anniversary, and I knew how much this trip meant to Mom. Besides, spending a few weeks at home wasn't so bad, especially for a homebody like me.

Mark was in town, and he offered to help me out. He

lives across the street, and my parents adore him. Mark is over 6 feet tall with dark brown hair and sky blue eyes. We were high school sweethearts. However, he's moving to California to attend Caltech in September, and I am going to stay local and attend Ohio State. They say long-distance relationships never work. So, I ended our relationship the night of the accident. Mark wasn't happy about it. He's been pining for me ever since.

We live in the suburbs outside of Columbus. Our home is quite spacious: 3 bedrooms, 2.5 baths, 2,500 square feet. What I love about the house is the small loft on top of the stairwell. I sort of made that area my mini-lounge. My mom had a huge collection of suspense stories that she let me keep. For several hours, I curled up on my futon and became immersed in a young adult thriller about a babysitter being threatened by a mysterious stranger when it happened: it was 3:33 PM, and my phone chimed to tell me that it sensed motion at the door. Dad installed this fancy motion sensor gadget to catch package thieves. "You can never be too careful," Dad always said.

With the clunky walking boot, I was in no condition to go running down the stairs. The app on my phone would have to do. When I loaded the app, I saw the front porch with a view of both the street and Mark's house. Nothing seemed out of the ordinary except that *there was no one at the door*. How could that be? The camera must have picked up *something*. That feeling was back. That feeling I had 6 weeks ago — *that night*.

I WOBBLED down the stairs as fast as I could and opened the door. I was startled by Mark.

"Hey! Wow — I didn't mean to scare you!" Mark exclaimed.

I was relieved to see Mark, but I paused to look around the porch area; again, nothing looked out of the ordinary.

"Mark, did you see anyone drop by?" I asked.

Mark shook his head. I looked back at the app on my phone; it indicated that there was a new motion, being that Mark was at the porch.

"Oh, you have that app that lets you know if there is motion at your door, huh? It's pretty cool," Mark said.

"Well, yeah, but I am a little confused. At 3:33, the app told me that someone was at the door. I didn't see anyone in the video. Can you look?"

I showed the video to Mark.

"Maybe it was just the breeze? It's been a bit windy today; maybe that set off the motion sensor?"

Mark investigated the doorbell and the device sensor. Nothing seemed out of the ordinary. But, how could it be?

"Not sure what to tell you, Jamie, but everything seems normal."

Everything did seem normal, and I was definitely feeling better now that Mark was there.

"Oh well. A false positive. No sense in worrying about it, right?" I shrugged. "Hey, why did you drop by, Mark?"

"Oh, no reason. Just wanted to see how you were doing. Your parents left for their trip, so I thought you could use some company."

Mark came into the house, and we settled on ordering a pizza and watching some TV. The History Channel was playing a special on ghosts. Parapsychologists discussed various theories, one of which proposed that apparitions are inter-dimensional beings who are living in another time and space: the multiverse theory, as it was called. In it, ghosts may simply be beings temporarily visible to us as dimensions get crossed up, giving us a glimpse into another world.

"Maybe that's what happened, Jamie? Maybe a being from another dimension rang your doorbell?" Mark smirked with amusement. He could be a smart ass at times. I shook my head at him.

"Seriously. In another dimension, you and I are not sitting on this couch but could be in Paris having a romantic stroll by the River Seine." Mark moved closer to me on the couch. "I could be leaning over to you like this."

Mark's blue eyes pierced into mine as he gently placed his hand on my face, slowly running his thumb on my lower lip. I could feel my heart beating faster. I never knew that Mark could be this romantic. Mark's lips were ready to touch mine when the doorbell rang. My phone buzzed indicating motion at the door. It was the pizza delivery guy.

MARK and I went back to watching TV and began eating the pizza. I wasn't brave enough to bring up what almost happened, and neither was Mark. Maybe it's for the best. I kept reminding myself that long distance relationships don't work. It's like what happened with my friend Shelly last summer. She met a really great guy who was visiting his cousins. They had a whirlwind romance for two months. He "promised" to write, and she "promised" to visit him over one of the breaks. It just wasn't meant to be, I guess.

Mark switched over to the local news. They run a special on Saturdays called *Missing* to discuss ongoing missing persons investigations in the area. There was a report of a girl, age 13, named Mary Montgomery of Edenvale. Her parents were unknown; her guardian, Ross Montgomery, came on the screen: a bearded man in his mid-50s who looked a bit like Obi-Wan Kenobi in the original *Star Wars*. It was the middle of the night, and Ross heard a loud thump in the hallway. He went over to check on Mary, but she had vanished. A photo of her appeared on the screen, and a chill came down my spine. She had pale skin and long, dark hair that seemed to cover her face slightly. She was wearing a white blouse and had an empty smile. Ross Montgomery indicated that he remembered that his clock had read 3:33 AM when he heard the thump on May 20th. My heart started to pound really fast, and I dropped my drink on the floor.

"Whoa! Hey, let me help you clean that up!" Mark reached over for some napkins. "Are you okay, Jamie? Looks like you saw a ghost."

"I think I just did," I said softly.

CHAPTER TWO

MAY 20, 2017

"I just can't do this Mark," I said with tears in my eyes.

"Jamie, I — I love you," Mark declared. "We have gone over this a hundred times. I am not going to give up on us. Yes, it's a chance of a lifetime to intern at the Jet Propulsion Lab. I have to see it through. But, I am coming back for you and will be here every summer. Please, please don't give up on us."

"I need time to think, Mark. I can't breathe right now." I ran over to my car as fast as I could. Mark tried to stop me, but it was too late as I sped off Shelly's driveway.

It began raining really hard. Mark had warned me that I needed to put some water repellent on the car. The windshield was so dirty. It was the first time it rained in a long time. Tears were still falling from my eyes.

"God, why is it so chilly?" I muttered to myself. I turned on the heater. It was the end of May for crying out loud. As I reached over for the heater, I accidentally tipped over the coffee sitting in my cup holder from earlier in the day.

"Dammit!" I yelled. I looked down briefly to see what damage I had done. Thankfully, the lid was still in place and nothing had spilt. When I looked up, however, there she was staring at me coldly from my rear-view mirror: a ghostly girl with dark hair covering her face.

I screamed in terror! Then, I swerved off the road and hit a large tree. My airbag went off. Before I blacked out, I glanced at the car clock as blood dripped down my face: 3:33 AM.

CHAPTER THREE

IT HAD TO BE MARY. I JUST KNOW IT. BUT WHY? How is it even possible?

"Hey, Jamie — you ok?" Mark looked over at me with deep concern.

"You aren't going to believe this, Mark, I — wait, it's just too improbable..." I couldn't believe I was actually thinking about it. Did I see a ghost?

"No, no. I need to know what's going on in there," Mark said, pointing at my head. "What is it, Jamie?"

"The girl. Mary Montgomery. I have *seen* her. She was — she was in the car with me the night of the accident. She just suddenly appeared and was staring at me from my rear-view mirror. Her face startled me. I don't know how she got into my car. She's what distracted me and made me hit the tree. She put me in this walking boot." I looked down at my fractured leg and began to cry.

"Shh, shh." Mark moved next to me and put his arm around my shoulder. "Jamie, look, there must be a logical explanation. Maybe she ran away from home? Maybe she hid in your car, and you didn't notice her? You were really angry at the party. You may have already been too distracted to notice that she was in your back seat — a stowaway."

It was nice being in Mark's arms. I did miss him. He always knows how to make me feel better.

"Jamie, look, maybe we should go to Edenvale tomorrow and talk to Ross Montgomery? We should tell him that you saw Mary. I know that you don't remember much, but maybe it can help solve some of the mystery?"

"Can you stay over tonight, Mark?" Mark nodded and continued to hold me. I kept having an unsettling feeling. It's been so cold in the house, as if there was *something* there.

MARK and I fell asleep on the living room sofa. Some infomercial aired on the TV and the lights were still on. My phone started to buzz. The buzzing woke me up, and my movement caused Mark to wake up.

"Oh wow. What time is it?" Mark asked while yawning and still half asleep.

I looked at my phone. It was 3:33 AM, and there was a message saying there was motion at the door. I played the video, and I screamed in terror! There was someone at the door: it was Mary Montgomery, covered in blood.

"Mark! *She's* at the door!" I shouted.

"Stay here, Jamie!" Mark rushed to the door with one of our fire-irons in his hand. He looked into the peephole, and there was no one there. Mark then opened the door. Still no one; just a breeze.

"Hey! Hey! Anyone there?" Mark yelled out. We could hear the dogs barking a few doors down. The neighborhood looked peaceful. Mark closed the door and locked it.

I was frozen on the couch. I couldn't move.

"Jamie, let me see your phone." I was speechless. Mark then discovered my phone on the floor. He looked at the video history, and there was *nothing*. Nothing since the pizza delivery guy.

"Jamie, I don't see the video. You *did* see a video, right?" Mark showed me the phone and the history. There was no video. I was in shock.

"Mark — Mark, I swear to you, there was a video. It was Mary Montgomery at the door. She was covered in blood! I'm not crazy, Mark." I started crying.

"You *aren't* crazy, Jamie. I believe you. You saw something. But, the video is gone. Could it be that you were having a nightmare?"

"No, Mark, it was *real*. And, Mark, 3:33 AM. AGAIN. 3:33 AM. Why, Mark? Why is this happening to me?"

CHAPTER FOUR

WE COULDN'T SLEEP, SO WE JUST TOOK OFF IN MARK'S
car and headed to Edenvale. My parents had texted me to
let me know they made it to Hawaii and were settled in.
Wifi would be spotty on the cruise ship, but they would
check-in when they could.

"Jamie, we are having a lot of connectivity issues," Dad
texted. "The doorbell app isn't loading video. We hope you
are okay."

I wasn't about to tell him about Mary Montgomery. I
wouldn't know where to begin.

Mark was driving and had turned the radio over to the
local news in case there were any reports even remotely
related to runaways, pranksters ... *something* to explain
what I had experienced.

"Breaking news: a body was discovered, badly decom-
posed. It appears to be that of a young girl. The speculation
is that it may be the body of 13-year old Mary Montgomery
of Edenvale, who has been missing since May 20. The

body was discovered about 15 miles north near Waverly Lake. Stay tuned to WKAM for the latest."

"Wait, that's near where you had your accident, Jamie!" Mark exclaimed. "We need to head up there, now!"

Mark made a u-turn and headed up the highway towards Waverly Lake.

———

IT DIDN'T TAKE LONG to find where the authorities were investigating the location of the young girl's body. We pulled over to the side of the road and proceeded as far as we could until we were stopped by the county Sheriff. I recognized him; he was the one who questioned me when I had my accident: Sheriff King.

Sheriff King was a portly man in his 50s. He was well-respected in the community, but he was known to have some unorthodox investigation techniques. His deputies joked that he was "Fox Mulder's redneck cousin."

"This is official law enforcement business. Head back to your car, kids," Sheriff King said sternly and only halfway paying attention to who we were.

"We apologize, Sheriff, but we have some information on Mary Montgomery," Mark stated firmly. "My girl — um — friend here believes she saw Mary the night of her disappearance."

The Sheriff looked over at us.

"Wait, I recognize you. You were the girl who ran into the tree; I think about 10 minutes down the road here." The Sheriff pointed up ahead.

"Yes, Sheriff King. My name is Jamie. I was distracted and ran into the tree. But, I think I know why. I saw Mary in my rear-view mirror. She must have been sitting in my back seat." Shivers came down my spine as I spoke those words.

"I know you were having problems remembering what happened to you that night, Miss Jamie," the Sheriff said. "It just doesn't seem possible based on everything we know about Mary." The Sheriff halted his conversation with us as the reporters were growing more anxious. "You'll have to excuse me, kids. If you want to make a statement, stop by my station later this afternoon, and we can talk then." The Sheriff walked toward the crowd that was gathering.

"There is something not right here, Jamie," Mark said. "We'll go by the station later, but let's see what we can find on our own in the meantime."

WE HEADED over to see if we could meet up with Ross Montgomery as originally planned.

There was only one Ross Montgomery listed for Edenvale. He lived in a modest neighborhood on Primrose Drive. There were police cars parked in his driveway, so it obviously wasn't the best time for us to chat with him. Instead, we parked down the road and began walking along the sidewalk. About 5 houses down, we saw two teenage girls most likely coming back from shopping, as they were carrying large department store bags. One girl was of legal driving age, maybe around 16, and the other, possibly her sister, looked about Mary's age. They gave us a wondering look as we walked down the sidewalk. Being one not to shy away from a conversation, Mark decided to engage with the young ladies.

"Excuse me. Do you happen to know someone named Mary Montgomery?" The two girls giggled a bit, taken aback by how handsome Mark was. I was used to it. He was definitely easy on the eyes.

"Yeah. Beth here went to school with her," the older girl said carefree. Beth blushed a little and then nodded at Mark and I.

"Beth, what can you tell us about Mary?" Mark asked without hesitation.

"Well, Mary didn't have many friends. She was skinny and awkward; the quiet type. Guess that's a deadly combination to become the butt of jokes." Beth looked a bit sad as she continued. "I talked to her now and then. I don't care what people think of me. I believe in the Golden Rule."

Beth continued. "The worst thing happened a week before school let out. Mary got her period. She was spotting like crazy and didn't know it. Someone played a prank on her. Kinda *Carrie*-esque. They stuffed her locker with tampons and wrote 'Bloody Mary' across her locker door."

I gasped. "My God, that's awful!"

"Yeah, the teachers were not happy," Beth said. "They couldn't prove who did it, though. They let Mary stay home for the remainder of the school year. And that's about all I know."

"Beth, Erica!" a voice from inside the adjacent house called out.

"Be right there, Mom," Erica said. "We have to get

going. Our mom is calling." Erica raced into the house. Beth headed to the door but then looked over at me for a second with a puzzled expression. She then shook it off and headed inside. As Beth walked in, I noticed a sign that said "Reese" above the front door. As I looked a little more carefully, I noticed that the house was equipped with the same doorbell monitor that I had; a chill went down my spine.

"Bloody Mary," Mark said, interrupting my thoughts. "Hey, don't you remember that game that you and I would play when we were younger? You had that old, creepy mirror in your attic, and we would go up there and speak the name 'Bloody Mary' into it three times in a row to see if we can summon a spirit. Remember that?"

"Yeah, I remember," I said. "Even though you said it never worked, I remember thinking I saw something appear the third time we tried. God, that really freaks me out, Mark, to think about it!"

———

I THINK I was around Mary's age when it happened. It was Halloween. I was dressed as a zombie bee, and Mark was a bee-keeper. Yes, we did silly things like that. It had been about 5 or more years since we played Bloody Mary. It never worked, but when Mark wanted to try this time, something felt a bit off. We were supposed to be asleep. It was really late at night. In fact, it could have been around 3 in the morning.

"No, Mark, I don't feel like playing," I said objectionably.

"Come on! It's Halloween. We are all entitled to one

good scare," Mark said convincingly. "Also, your parents plan to have a garage sale and most of the stuff in the attic are going away. Let's give the mirror one last try!"

As thirteen-year-olds, we were beginning to develop feelings for each other. Innocent crushes, but we knew something was there. Mark's charm made it easy for him to persuade me to play along.

"All right, but I really am getting tired."

Carrying a lighter and some candles, we climbed up to the attic where my parents stored the old mirror. It was very tall, about 7 feet. It looked like something out of *Harry Potter*. It was a family heirloom, passed on by my great-great-grandmother. Rumor has it that she was a heretic. My dad, being the scientist he was, didn't believe in "hocus pocus." So the mirror was placed in the attic to be sold off one day with all the other "pieces of junk."

Mark lit the candles. I saw our reflection in the mirror; two kids in their costumes. As I looked closer at my reflection, I thought I saw something behind me; a shadow of sorts. I gasped and quickly looked behind me. Of course, nothing was there, and I gathered my breath.

"Hey, you ok?" Mark asked with concern.

"Yeah." I shook it off but still felt a bit unsettled.

"Okay. Then let's begin," Mark said in a serious tone. "Let's say it together ... 1, 2, 3..."

"Bloody Mary," we said calmly together.

"Bloody Mary," we chanted again. The attic temperature felt like it dropped a few degrees.

After a slight pause, Mark and I looked at each other then turned to the mirror.

"Bloody Mary."

To Mark's disappointment, all that appeared in the mirror were our reflections.

"Dammit," Mark said disappointingly. "Come on, Jamie. Guess it's a night of tricks rather than treats." Mark began walking back to the ladder.

"Hey wait, we need to blow out the candles." As I looked back to blow them out, there she was. Her face was as white as snow, and she had blood-red lips. I screamed at the top of my lungs and passed out on the floor.

The next morning, I woke up in bed. According to Mark, he thinks the scream came from me tripping over the rug on the attic floor and burning my hand on one of the candles. I was known to be a bit clumsy. My parents scolded us for being up in the attic so late by ourselves. They had their garage sale, and the mirror was picked up by someone from out of town. No one believed that I saw anything; after a while, I became convinced that I didn't see anything either. Until now...

<hr>

"WELL, I believed I saw *something* in the mirror that night, Mark," I said sadly.

"Something did happen, Jamie," Mark said. "And maybe all of this is tied together. You know I am the practical type, a lot like your dad. There has to be a logical explanation to it all. Let's grab a bite to eat and head over to the Sheriff's station. We can tell him everything we know, and let's see if any of this adds up."

I thought that was a good idea, and we took off to downtown. Beth looked out of her bedroom window at our passing car. She then turned around and took out her hairbrush. She walked over and looked at her reflection in the antique 7-foot tall mirror that her family acquired in a garage sale 5 years before and smiled.

CHAPTER FIVE

MARK AND I HEADED OVER TO OUR FAVORITE BURGER joint and grabbed some sliders. It was good comfort food considering what we had gone through in the last 24 hours.

"Hey, did you notice that Beth and Erica have the same doorbell monitor that I have?" I asked Mark.

"Yeah, now that I think about it, I saw that, too," Mark said with his mouth full. "Beth said she knew Mary from school. You know, let me see if she has a Facebook page. Beth Reese of Edenvale..."

Mark took out his phone and browsed through various Facebook profiles and found Beth. It was a selfie of she and Erica. Beth had some public wall posts. In fact, one was from yesterday, around 3:40 PM: it read, "This motion monitor sucks. It tells me someone is at the door, but look..." She shared the video from her phone. There was no one at the door. The timestamp was 3:33 PM.

"Oh my God! What time is it now?" I asked Mark frantically.

"It's almost 3:30 PM now. I wonder..." Mark's sentence

was interrupted by a buzz from my phone. A motion detection ... at 3:33 PM.

"Oh no, Mark!" I didn't dare to look at my phone.

"Give me your phone," Mark demanded. I handed it over to him. A pale look came over his face. "What the hell?"

I had to look. I moved next to Mark and saw the video. A piece of paper was blowing in the wind. The paper blew in front of the camera and read "BETH" in blood red.

"We need to go back and see Beth. *Now*."

BETH WAS IN HER ROOM, fully satisfied after the big meal that her mom cooked. The girls' mom had to leave the house to pick up their father, as his car was in the shop. Beth put on her headphones. She was drifting to sleep but was awakened by a series of tapping noises, as if someone was tapping on glass. Beth removed her headphones and looked around. She didn't see anything out of the ordinary. Her window was open to let in a breeze and everything looked to be in place. Shrugging it off, Beth put her headphones back on. The tapping grew louder, and then there was a voice, a woman's voice: "Beth..."

Beth shot out of her bed and screamed, "Who's there?!" Her heart was racing and her breathing grew harder. Nothing. There was no one in the room. Terrified, Beth raced to her bedroom door only to find that she couldn't open it. It was jammed. The tapping continued, and the voice grew louder: "Beth..."

Now Beth realized where the sound was coming from.

Beth was facing the door and very slowly turned her head to view the mirror in the room...

WE RACED to Beth's house. Fortunately, we didn't get a speeding ticket. Mark jumped out of the car. With my walking boot on, I hobbled as fast as I could to the front door. Mark rang the doorbell and knocked really hard.

"Coming..." Erica's voice didn't sound anxious or concerned.

"Erica, hurry up! It's Mark and Jamie. From earlier..." Mark stated in panic.

Erica opened the door, and Mark raced inside.

"Beth! Beth!" Mark shouted.

"Whoa — wait, what's going on?" Erica's eyes were wide open with concern.

"We are afraid something could be wrong with Beth. Where is she?" Mark asked.

"She should be upstairs in her room," Erica said with a very confused look on her face.

Mark ran up the stairs. Erica and I followed as fast as we could.

"Oh my God!" Mark shouted. Beth's door was open, and she was unconscious on the floor. Her left arm was exposed, and there appeared to be marks burned into her skin, as if *someone* grabbed her arm and squeezed it with something that was red hot.

"Beth! Beth!" Erica cried out as she ran over to her sister. Slowly Beth regained consciousness. Erica and Mark picked Beth up and moved her onto her bed. Erica told me to grab some cream and a washcloth from the bathroom down the hall. I returned with the items and a cup of tap water. Erica thanked me and had Beth take a small sip of water. As Beth sipped her water, she whispered, "Mirror."

"Mirror?" Mark questioned.

"The mirror," Beth said more deliberately.

I glanced around and noticed that there was a large object behind the door; it looked familiar. I looked behind the door to see the same 7-foot mirror that had been in my parents' attic!

"Mark! It's my parents' old mirror!" I shouted.

Mark came over and stared at it.

"When did you get this mirror?" Mark asked Erica.

"My parents bought it in an antique sale about 5 years ago, I think," Erica explained. "For some reason, Beth was mesmerized by it, so Mom and Dad let her have it."

"The mirror..." Beth said again.

"Yes, Beth, what happened?" Erica asked gently.

"I — I don't remember. Ouch." Beth felt the burn marks. "I just remember that I saw something in the mirror and then blacked out."

The mirror didn't look out of the ordinary. It was maybe just a bit more worn than might be expected.

"How did you know to come back here and that Beth was in trouble?" Erica asked with concern on her face.

Mark looked over at me, as if hesitant to explain the situation, but he continued.

"Jamie has a motion detector, just like the one you have installed in your house, at her place. It was set off today, and a piece of paper came flying onto the screen that said 'BETH.' Do you have the video, Jamie?"

I took out my phone, and loaded the app, but the video was gone! I gasped.

"Mark! The video is gone!"

Mark grabbed my phone, and the last video was the pizza guy at the door from last night.

"Erica, Beth. We swear to you. There was a video..." Mark was stopped mid-sentence by Erica.

"I think you both should leave," Erica said with a suspicious look. "Our parents are going to be home soon." She looked over at her sister, who still seemed in shock.

"Something is not right here. We want to help," I pleaded.

"No, please go. We appreciate your concern, but please," Erica said boldly.

We honored her wishes and walked out of the house.

"This is crazy, Mark. I feel like this is one big nightmare."

"Let's go see Sheriff King," Mark said sternly. "We need to get to the bottom of this."

AS WE PULLED into the station, Sheriff King arrived simultaneously. We stopped him as he got out of his vehicle.

"Sheriff! We need to speak with you now!" Mark urged. "We have some very important information about the Mary Montgomery case."

"Okay, son, calm down," Sheriff King said while patting Mark on the shoulder. "You and Miss Jamie here can come inside my office, and we can chat."

We sat down in Sheriff King's office. It was a medium-sized office. He had a library of books about sociopaths, unsolved murders, small-town crimes ... and one that stood out in particular was titled *Hanako-San: Myth or Reality?*

Mark and I went into detail about the events of the last day and a half. The Sheriff didn't look at all suspicious about what we were telling him. In fact, he seemed intrigued.

"Beth Reese," Sheriff King muttered. "Well, we questioned her when Mary disappeared. She told you that she befriended Mary? Well, that's not what we gathered. We have some reason to believe that she may have been the mastermind behind the 'Bloody Mary' incident."

Mark and I looked at each other in amazement.

"Beth is very popular at the school. She's been known to be kind of mean. My son goes to school with Erica, and he has seen how the two girls behave. They tend to make fun of others who are a little awkward, like Mary was.

"Mr. Reese, the girls' father, is the Principal at the school, and there is a chance he knew that Beth was guilty of the bullying. This is all speculation. We don't have any proof. I mean, I shouldn't even tell you what I am telling you right now.

"Now, this incident regarding the mirror and the burn marks... Well, I owe the Reeses a visit. I'll see what I can gather."

"What do you think this all means, Sheriff?" I asked. "I mean, everything that happened with my accident, the videos, the mirror... Is there a logical explanation?"

The Sheriff turned his head over to his library of books. "Miss Jamie, as you can see, I read a lot of books on unsolved mysteries and even on the occult. I do believe you experienced *something*. Hopefully, there is a logical explanation."

The Sheriff took down our contact information and said he would give us a call. He seemed to sympathize with us. We definitely wouldn't expect him to share as much as he did, as this was an on-going investigation. However, he was as keen as we were to get this mystery solved.

CHAPTER SIX

MAY 14, 2017

"MARY, IT'S TIME TO GET READY FOR SCHOOL!" ROSS Montgomery blurted from the kitchen.

Mary Montgomery, at age 13, had gone through more than anyone her age could imagine. She never knew her mother and father; she only knew the Montgomerys. Ross worked from home as a graphic designer. He was a loving man and did the best he could to raise Mary as his own. He and his wife were unable to have children, so they adopted Mary when she was 4. When Mary turned 7, Ross's wife, Grace, died of ovarian cancer at 45 years old. She left the family with a small amount of savings from an inheritance she had received. This was money that Ross set aside for Mary to use to go to college.

Mary never asked for much. She missed Grace, but Ross was a responsible and attentive guardian. He wasn't exactly the most fashionable man, and he didn't keep up on the latest pop culture trends. So, Mary naturally tended to follow his lead. At school, the girls would pick on her because she appeared uncomfortable in her own skin. Mary was thin and wasn't developing at the rate of many others, like Beth Reese, for example. Mary's big green eyes seemed much larger than her face.

Mary put on some jeans and a white shirt with a floral pattern. She went downstairs, and Ross handed her a bag with her lunch. He kissed her on the cheek, and she walked over to the bus stop.

The sky was gray that morning. There was only about a week remaining for the school year. Along the route to the bus stop was the cemetery where Grace was buried. Out of the corner of her eye, Mary thought she saw someone: a mysterious woman wearing white. Maybe it was someone visiting a grave? The woman looked over at Mary. It was hard to see the woman's expression, but it gave Mary chills. Luckily, the bus arrived, and Mary hopped on as quickly as possible.

There was chatter as usual on the bus, and Mary sat alone as always — on the last seat in the back right side of the bus. Today felt a tad off. Mary began feeling dizzy and her stomach was cramping. Could it have been from breakfast? It was hard to tell. It was an unfamiliar feeling.

The bus stopped at the school, and Mary headed out. Beth Reese and her friends were talking about boys and playing on their smartphones. As Mary walked by, Beth and her friends looked up at her, turned to each other and started whispering and laughing. Mary just ignored them and headed to class. What Mary didn't realize was that she started spotting on her pants. Beth and her friends' laughing grew louder. Everyone outside stared at Mary and others joined in on the laughter when they noticed the bleeding. Still oblivious, Mary walked into the building. Mrs. Johnson was at her desk when she saw Mary walk in. She noticed the problem right away.

"Mary, dear, oh my! Looks like you have your period." Mrs. Johnson reached over into her desk and pulled out a maxi pad. "Here, dear, head to the ladies' room."

Mary felt so embarrassed. It all made sense to her now. She rushed into the bathroom, and Mrs. Johnson followed to make sure Mary was okay.

"I can call your father, and you can go home for the day."

Mary came out from the stall and nodded her head in agreement with Mrs. Johnson.

"I'll be right outside," Mrs. Johnson said.

Mary turned on the faucet, looking down in shame, tears continuing to pour down her face. When Mary looked up into the mirror, eyes foggy from the tears, she could have sworn she saw another girl staring back at her. She wasn't anyone Mary had recognized; she was very pale, had dark hair and black eyes. She was holding a brown, worn teddy bear. She put her index finger to her lips.

"Shhhhh!" the girl said.

Mary quickly turned around, and there was no one there; no one in any stalls either.

"You're imagining things, Mary," she thought.

Mrs. Johnson greeted Mary. She didn't think to bring up the girl in the mirror; there was already too much chaos.

"Can I go to my locker first? I need to take home some books," Mary said quietly.

Students scrambled to their first class of the day as

Mrs. Johnson walked with Mary to her locker. Mrs. Johnson gasped in horror. There it was ... in blood red: "BLOODY MARY" written boldly across Mary's locker. The door was ajar and tampons were flowing out from it. Students laughed as they slowly passed by for a better look, and the Principal, Mr. Reese, rushed over to break up the crowd.

"Settle down! Who is responsible for this?" Mr. Reese asked sternly. The laughter turned to silence. "Head to your classes now! Mary, walk with me."

Mr. Reese brought Mary and Mrs. Johnson to his office. Mary was speechless. She was hurt and angry. She had never felt this much rage before. She saw Beth Reese out of the corner of her eye. Beth's laughter came to a halt as she felt a chill down her spine when she saw the anger in Mary's eyes.

———

"MR. MONTGOMERY, we are going to get to the bottom of this fiasco," Mr. Reese assured Ross Montgomery, as he held Mary in his arms.

"You'd better get control of your students," Ross scolded. "I'll take this to the school board if I have to."

Ross and Mary walked out of Mr. Reese's office and headed out to their car.

As Ross started driving, he noticed how quiet Mary was.

"Mary, I can't believe how mean kids can be," Ross explained. "I can say that things will get better. I mean, back when I was in high school, I was picked on by the star basketball captain. Today, he's between jobs and has to find a way to provide child support for 3 children!"

Mary appreciated that Ross attempted to make her feel better, but she didn't feel like talking. She had a strong suspicion Beth was the mastermind behind the prank. Maybe Beth will get what's coming to her, she thought to herself.

CHAPTER SEVEN

MAY 19, 2017

It had been a few days since the "Bloody Mary" incident. Mary wouldn't leave her room; she would spend the day in bed, periodically crying. Several family portraits sat on Mary's nightstand. Her favorite was a photo of Grace when she visited London. Grace had long, dark hair and a warm, beautiful smile.

"Why do the good ones get taken from us so soon?" Mary thought aloud.

The Montgomerys were not religious people; Ross considered himself agnostic, and Grace considered herself a "spiritual" person. Since Grace's passing, and as Mary grew older, the idea crossed her mind that maybe once you are gone you are really, truly gone: just a dark emptiness. If that was the case, then everything was insignificant, Mary conceded. Who cares about anything, really?

Mary climbed out of bed and walked to her window. It was a hazy, sunny day with a slight breeze. The leaves were rustling in the wind. For just a moment, Mary thought she could hear Grace's voice as the wind blew. It sounded like she was gently calling out "Mary." Mary shivered, but she shrugged it off.

"Just my imagination," Mary whispered.

Mary felt the need to go to the cemetery to visit Grace. She put on the summer hat that Grace used to wear and proceeded down the stairs to see Ross taking a nap. Normally, she went with Ross to visit Grace. Ross worked so hard, and he looked so peaceful. It was nice to see him take a quick break, which was the beauty of being able to work from home. Mary quietly snuck out through the back door.

"I won't be gone very long," Mary thought out loud. Ross would definitely be worried if she was, but Mary really wanted to just go on her own. She seemed drawn to do so, like something or *someone* called to her.

THE CEMETERY WAS one of the oldest in the state. It was built during the Civil War. You can find headstones of Union lieutenants. For example, Adam Coleman, 2nd Lieutenant with Co D, 4th West Virginia Infantry Regiment; enlisted June 24, 1861. Mary knew some Civil War history from her social studies and civics classes: a nation divided. It's not much different from school, Mary thought: the Beth Reeses of the world oppressing, dividing...

Mary was deep in thought when she saw her again: the woman from a few days ago, wandering about the cemetery, about 100 yards away. She was a woman most likely in her late-30s with very long dark hair and a pale complexion.

She was wearing a white gown, something you might wear to bed. She stopped and stared at Mary.

"Hello?" Mary asked. "Can I help you?"

The woman began to place her hand on her stomach and bent over. She seemed to be in pain.

Mary ran over to her to see if she could help.

CHAPTER EIGHT

MARK AND I DECIDED THAT MAYBE WE COULD TRY ROSS Montgomery again, so we headed back to Primrose Drive. With all the excitement, I never noticed the old cemetery down the road. Out of the corner of my eye, I could have sworn I saw a dark-haired woman in white wandering past the graves.

"Hey, Mark. Let's stop here," I urged.

"Why do you want to visit this place?" Mark asked.

"I think I saw something," I claimed.

We parked along the street and headed into the cemetery. We saw old gravestones dating back to the Civil War. There were newer sections as well. People were still laid to rest here. As we were walking, I saw her: the woman in white.

"Mark! Look! There she is." I pointed over to the woman.

"Hello?" Mark asked the woman.

The woman did not reply back. In fact, she just ignored us and continued to walk away. We headed over to where we found her, but we stopped abruptly to find a summer hat on the ground jarred next to some bushes and a headstone: Grace Montgomery, Loving Wife and Mother.

I gasped, "Mary..."

Before I could say anything else, Mark's phone began to ring. It was Sheriff King.

"Kids, you'd better head back down to the station," Sheriff King said. "I have an important update that I think you all need to hear. It's best done in person."

WE HEADED BACK to the Sheriff's station to be greeted immediately by Sheriff King. He took us back to his office and shut the door behind him.

"Well, I have some big news: Mary may still be alive!" Sheriff King exclaimed. "Seems the body was not of Mary but another girl who had been missing, a runaway."

Mark and I looked at each other in shock and wonder.

"And that's not everything," Sheriff King added. "I visited the Reese's home. The girls told me about the incident. Jamie, the mirror in Beth's room, that was in your family? What do you know about it?"

I was taken aback by the line of questioning, but I answered the best I could.

"Well, it came from my dad's family," I explained. "They have lived in the area for generations. There was a rumor that my great-great-grandmother was a heretic."

"Well, I can confirm that your great-great-grandmother, Margaret, was not a heretic," Sheriff King said in a serious tone. "Were you aware that she was not your great-great-grandfather's first wife?"

I looked up at Sheriff King, puzzled.

"That's news to me," I said curiously.

Sheriff King continued. "Well, there's a very bizarre story regarding the mirror and your ancestors. It's a bit tough to hear, but with everything that's going on, I think you need to learn the whole story. I uncovered these details from an old investigation that happened in this very county back in the early 1900s.

"Your great-great-grandfather, Elias Patterson, age 25, came to Edenvale, Ohio with no money but big ambitions as an inventor. He had befriended an older woman named Rosa Hunter, age 45, and they wed very quickly, after only 1 month of meeting. Rosa was widowed and gained a bit of wealth through her late husband. She had a daughter. Her name was Mary, age 13."

Mark and I looked at each other in wonder as Sheriff King continued.

"Rosa was very jealous of young Mary. She could see that Mary was growing into a very beautiful young woman. Not only did she have outer beauty, but she also had a strong will and was very caring. When Elias seemed to gravitate towards Mary, Rosa felt threatened and locked Mary in the attic for hours. There was a large mirror in the attic, and Mary would find herself trapped. She would beg her mother to let her out, but Rosa would keep Mary in the attic for hours, up until when Elias would arrive home. Rosa threatened Mary to never tell Elias what happened or there would be 'severe consequences.'"

"Oh my God," Mark interrupted. "This is terrible. Did Rosa ever get reported to the authorities?"

"She got what was coming to her," Sheriff King added with a smirk.

"One fateful day, Mary encountered Hanako-San. I don't know if you kids have noticed, but I have a book about this urban legend in my collection. Hanako-San is the Japanese legend of a little girl who haunts bathrooms. Seems Mary claimed, however, that Hanako-San appeared in the attic mirror. There is thought that the legend went beyond just haunting bathrooms: the spirit would torment young women in pain via any type of mirror.

"Elias would be working on his inventions very late at night in the outdoor shed that he turned into a workshop. Mary and Rosa got into a final argument, why so late at night, no one knows. It was so bad that it was heard by several neighbors. Rosa chased Mary up into the attic. Elias heard the commotion and ran up the stairs to stop it. Two concerned neighbors also joined Elias. When they got up to the attic, Rosa was there all alone: Mary had vanished. The time was 3:33 AM!

"Rosa pleaded to investigators that something came out of the mirror in the attic and grabbed Mary. No one believed her. There was enough town speculation that Rosa had been abusing Mary. Rosa and Elias divorced shortly after the disappearance of Mary. Mary Hunter's disappearance is one of our most infamous cold cases.

"From our records, Rosa was shamed and left town. She ended up passing away from a mysterious illness a few years later while living in Vermont. Elias moved to Columbus and met your blood great-great-grandmother.

Jamie, you probably never learned about the Mary Hunter case, as Elias and Rosa's marriage records were destroyed in the Edenvale City Hall Fire of 1906."

Mark and I were left speechless. I had chills running down my spine. I started rubbing my arms, as I was feeling very cold.

"I told you all this was a lot to absorb," Sheriff King said, concerned. "Kids, I know you claimed that there were videos of Mary Montgomery. The camera you have at home, Jamie... I had one of my deputies stop by your house, and he looked at the model installed: it contains a mirror to help provide a wider view of the porch. I know this sounds crazy, and they call me the 'redneck Fox Mulder' around here, so I'll just say it: I think Mary Montgomery was taken by Hanako-San, or as you kids call her, 'Bloody Mary!'"

CHAPTER NINE

MAY 19, 2017 @ 7 PM

"MARY, DINNER TIME!" ROSS HAD SUPPER READY. ROSS overslept and didn't hear Mary come back from her cemetery walk. When he woke up, Mary was sound asleep in bed.

When Mary didn't answer him, Ross put down the plates and headed up the stairs. Mary's door was closed.

"Knock, knock. Can I come in?" Ross asked.

"Come in," Mary said gently.

When Ross opened the door, Mary was dressed very peculiarly: all in white. The dress looked vintage, like something out of the early 1900s.

"Okay... new dress? When did you get that?" Ross asked.

"Oh, it's been in my closet," Mary said nonchalantly as she combed her long, dark hair and stared into the mirror by her dresser.

"Well, kids and their fashions, I guess. And, I know you have been through a lot," Ross shrugged.

"I have dinner ready. Come down when you are done with 'dress up,'" Ross said sarcastically.

When Ross left, Mary began smiling; not a pretty, healthy smile, but one of mischief. The person on the other side of the mirror was not Mary Montgomery. It was Mary Hunter, covered in blood, with Hanako-San behind her.

———

THE GRADUATION PARTY was running really late; over 50 guests. It began at 7 PM, and now it was almost 2 AM on May 20. I can't believe how much energy everyone had. I'll probably be the most boring Freshman at Ohio State; falling asleep while everyone else is just starting their evenings.

I've known Shelly for as long as I can remember. She is a thin Indian girl with long black hair and about my height. Shelly's parties were always infamous for bringing out the wild side in people. She's been hosting gatherings since, well, her 5th birthday party.

Mark held me close to him all night. We looked like the perfect couple as always: "peas in a pod," they say. Why does he have to leave? I need him. I really do. I'll feel empty without him.

I needed some time to think. I excused myself and went to the bathroom. While I was away, Mark, Shelly, Shelly's younger sister Misha and Mark's friend Steve started joking aloud.

"Hey, Jamie and I used to play this game called 'Bloody Mary.' It was a total trip!" Mark was a bit tipsy. Yes, we weren't supposed to be drinking, but someone "happened" to add an extra element to one of the bowls of punch.

"I totally know that game!" Shelly interjected. "You know, guys, we can try it now. I have a long mirror in my room; come on!"

———

IT WAS ALMOST 3:30 AM. Ross had been tossing and turning all night.

"God, that dinner with Mary was so off," he thought. She seemed like a totally different person; not the sweet girl he raised but someone who had confidence in a disturbing sort of way.

It was just too unsettling for Ross. He decided to get up and take a peek to see if Mary was sleeping peacefully.

THUD!

Ross rushed into Mary's room.

"MARY!!!! MARY!!!! Oh, God!"

The clock read 3:33 AM.

CHAPTER TEN

"There's got to be a way to stop all of this, Sheriff." My voice was shaking as I said those words.

"Kids, I think there is a way," Sheriff King said. "One of these mirrors is the conduit. I suspect it's the one in Beth Reese's house. However, this is very dangerous. We want to get Mary Montgomery out of there alive."

"Alive?" Mark asked. "How do we even know Mary is truly alive? There is something evil here, Sheriff. And, I'm a practical man of science. I still feel that we are dealing with forces beyond our control."

"According to the Hanako-San legend, the victim is put into a trance," Sheriff King interjected. "There hasn't been a new 'victim' yet, as Beth Reese was able to escape. So, if we can get Mary out of there, she can be set free. Her physical body is *in* the mirror. Think of it as a portal to another dimension."

"So the secret is the *timing*," I added. "Think about it. 3:33. All the events happen at this specific time in the early morning or afternoon. Could we find a way to pull Mary out of the mirror?"

"There's only one way to find out." Sheriff King called to one of his deputies. "We are going to head over to the Reese house around 3 AM. The Reeses will be set up at a hotel. We'll wait for 3:33 AM, and get Mary out of there and keep the evil 'Marys' in the other dimension. Kids, we will set you up at the hotel, too."

WE ENTERED the car with Deputy Scott, a handsome man, maybe in his early-30s, muscular build, with dark hair and eyes. He was assigned to drive us to the hotel, which was about 5 blocks from the Reese home.

"All this 'Bloody Mary' mess is our fault," I explained to Mark. "Why did we play that silly game? I can't just let these good officers risk their lives for something we may have caused."

"Jamie, if you go, I go, too."

"Kids, you heard what Sheriff King said. This is for law enforcement to handle," Deputy Scott said sternly.

I shrugged at Mark, but he and I were both thinking the same thing: we'll find a way to the Reese house.

IT WAS 3 AM. Deputy Scott was still in his car and was messaging someone on his phone. From the smile on his face, it was probably a girlfriend. He didn't see us sneak by him. Mark and I headed on foot over to the Reese residence. Of course, I was still wobbling in my walking boot, but we hoped to get there before 3:33 AM.

We passed by the old cemetery again.

"Mark, remember that lady we saw at the cemetery?" I asked.

Mark nodded.

"Do you think she's tied into this somehow? I mean, we don't know much about Mary Hunter and Hanako-San."

"Possibly," Mark added. "Definitely a mysterious person, but I don't know where to find her. Hard to tell anything in the cemetery when it's dark."

As we walked past, we didn't notice, but she was there, next to Grace's marker.

SHERIFF KING and his team set up shop in Beth's room. They lit candles around the mirror. Based on the Hanako-San legend, the conduit can be closed by breaking the mirror. They had a sledgehammer ready to hit as soon as they would be able to get Mary out of the mirror. Ross Montgomery waited behind the officers, hoping and praying Mary was still alive and well.

We were able to sneak in through the front door and climbed up the stairs to see the Sheriff and his team bracing for 3:33 AM. The mirror in the room began to liquify. Mary Montgomery's hand slowly began to appear when my phone started buzzing. Someone or *something* was at *my door*!

"Oh my God, Mark!" I exclaimed.

"Kids! What are you doing here?!" Sheriff King yelled while trying to grab onto Mary's hand.

Mark and I quickly watched the video. It was a note floating in blood-red letters: "JAMIE."

I dropped my phone and passed out on the floor.

EPILOGUE

THE BLOODY MARY INCIDENT WAS OVER. WHEN I passed out, Sheriff King was able to grab Mary Montgomery out of the mirror. His team was able to destroy the mirror before anything or *anyone* else could come out.

Days had passed; no mysterious video alerts: just the pizza guy, Mark ... and then my parents when they got back from Hawaii. Strangely, none of the mysterious videos loaded on my parents' phones. Needless to say, Mark and I kept the Bloody Mary incident to ourselves.

Sheriff King commended Mark and I on our bravery. Mary Montgomery was safe and had no recollection of the events. The last thing she remembered was visiting Grace at the cemetery. Beth learned her lesson: she was not "above" anyone else. The Sheriff's department decided to keep under wraps the "Bloody Mary" portion of the case. Instead, they said that Mary simply ran away and came back.

We were safe.

SHELLY and I became roommates at Ohio State. Most of Shelly's furniture arrived today. Mark went to Caltech as planned, but, of course, we got back together. I mean, who can resist those sky blue eyes?

"Sweetie, I'm heading to the library," I told Mark on our video call.

"I miss you! Remember, I'll be over there in a few weeks." Mark blew me a virtual kiss. I grabbed it in the air and placed it near my heart.

There was some thunder crackling outside. Looks like a storm was coming. The clock read 12:33 PM on Mark's end. I keep forgetting he's 3 hours behind me. We ended our video call.

"Time to get ready for the library," I thought. I needed to fix my hair and put on a rain jacket. I closed the door behind me, as we had just added the large door mirror that Shelly brought over from her house. When I looked in the mirror, it was clear I wasn't alone. *She* was there: Bloody Mary, standing right behind me...

ABOUT THE AUTHOR

Growing up loving horror and mystery tales, JC Bratton writes stories that pay homage to the Point Horror novels she would read as a kid: stories such as *Slumber Party* by Christopher Pike and *Twisted* by RL Stine. Some of her biggest influences are Alfred Hitchcock, Lois Duncan, Stephen King, and Richard Matheson.

Although she hopes for that Netflix movie deal, JC still has her day job and lives in the heart of Silicon Valley with her husband, stepsons, and cats.

amazon.com/author/jcbratton

youtube.com/@jcbratton

ABOUT BLUE MILK PUBLISHING

Blue Milk Publishing represents independent authors of both fiction and non-fiction works.

*Please visit **bluemilk.co** for more information.*

Non-Fiction

The Cheating Boyfriend (And Other Organizational Indiscretions) (January 2017) by Jenny Hayes Carhart, MSOD, PHR

Fiction

Who's at the Door? (January 2020) by JC Bratton

Parasomnia (June 2020) by JC Bratton

Dollhouse (October 2020) by JC Bratton

Who's Back at the Door? (October 2023) by JC Bratton

JC Bratton's Things That Go Bump in the Night, Volume One: Urban Legends (October 2023) by JC Bratton